SILLI'S SHEEP

written by **Tiffany Stone**

illustrated by **Louis Thomas**

schwartz & wade books · new york

In a mountain meadow, in the open air,
lived a man named Silli.

All day he frolicked in the sunshine, while
at night he needed nothing but moonbeams
for a bed.

Then one morning, a gust of wind paid
a visit. It was there only a moment, but
still, Silli felt . . . chilly.

Brrrr!

The next morning, the wind visited again.
What if it came to stay?

Silli searched in his sack for a solution.

Nothing.

He sighed and scanned the sky.

"Sheep!" he exclaimed, pointing to the clouds. "That's what I need. Sheep to make wool . . . wool to make yarn . . . yarn to make a sweater to keep me warm."

Silli wasn't a shepherd, but he was sure he could find some sheep.

Silli looked high.

And Silli looked low.
Where were the sheep?

Aha!

Up on a hill, Silli spotted . . . one sheep.
Two sheep. Three sheep. Four. Five.
Five sheep to make wool, to make yarn,
to make a sweater to keep him warm.

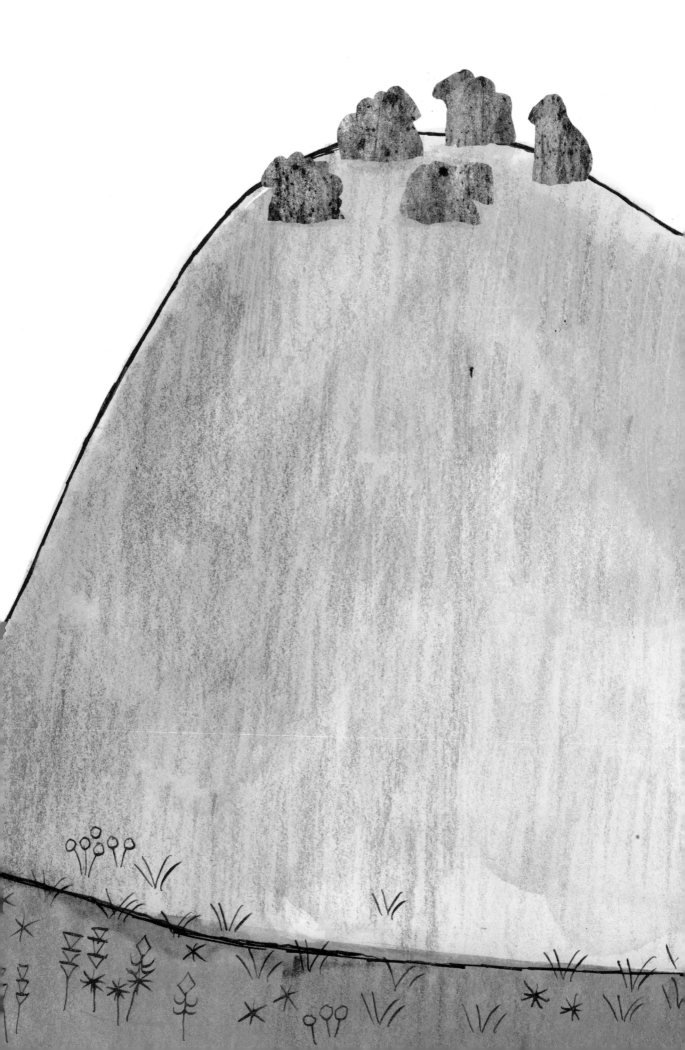

Silli hurried over and
hiked up to the top.

"Follow me, sheep!" he said.
But the sheep didn't move.

Not even when Silli tempted them
with handfuls of hay.
Not even when he showed them
how delicious it was.

Silli was stumped. "Shifting sheep is rough," he said. "Rough, rough, rough!"

Silli giggled. He sounded like a dog!

"Oh," said Silli, "that's what I need! A sheepdog to round up my sheep."

Silli looked high.

And Silli looked low.

He even searched in his sack.
But Silli didn't have a sheepdog—just like he didn't have wool or yarn or a sweater to keep him warm if the wind came to stay.

"I know what to do!" exclaimed Silli.

The sheep *still* didn't move.

So, one by one, Silli picked them up
and carried them down the hill.

They were very heavy.
"What *have* you been
eating?" Silli asked.

Once his flock was comfortably settled, Silli
took out his sharpest shears. Soon he would have
everything he needed to make his sweater.
Except there was a problem. . . .
Their wool was as hard as stone.

"Not to worry," said Silli. "I know what to do."

He squirted on conditioner and squeezed on lotion.
He even mashed up the bananas he was saving for
later and smeared them on the sheep.

But their wool was *still* as hard as stone.

And so, the very next day, when the wind did come to stay, Silli had no wool, no yarn, and no warm sweater. Just five impossible sheep.

The wind whirled around Silli, chilling his face, his arms, his feet.

But my back isn't chilly, thought Silli. *Why is that?*

When Silli turned around, he knew.
"Thank you," he said, giving the wind-
shielding sheep a hug.

A smile spread across Silli's chilly
lips. "I know what to do."

"My side isn't chilly!"
Silli's smile grew even wider.

Silli added another sheep.

And another.

Silli wasn't chilly anymore.

"I don't need a sweater," he declared. "I don't need yarn. I don't even need wool. I just need sheep.
"And maybe a cow. To make hot chocolate . . ."

To Cameron, sheep counter extraordinaire,
and Liam, the best test reader ever. You rock! –T.S.

To my silly Jade, with love –L.T.

Text copyright © 2020 by Tiffany Stone
Jacket art and interior illustrations copyright © 2020 by Louis Thomas

Visit us on the Web! rhcbooks.com

Educators and librarians, for a variety of teaching tools, visit us at RHTeachersLibrarians.com

Library of Congress Cataloging-in-Publication Data
Names: Stone, Tiffany, author. | Thomas, Louis, illustrator.
Title: Silli's sheep / by Tiffany Stone; illustrated by Louis Thomas.
Description: First edition. | New York: Schwartz & Wade Books, 2020. | Audience: Ages 3–7. | Audience: Grades K–1.
Summary: As winter nears, Silli wants wool to knit a sweater but the "sheep" he finds are actually stones,
so getting them home and sheared will be a challenge.
Identifiers: LCCN 2019028303 | ISBN 978-1-9848-4852-9 (hardback)
ISBN 978-1-9848-4853-6 (library binding) | ISBN 978-1-9848-4854-3 (ebook)
Subjects: CYAC: Fools and jesters—Fiction. | Sheep—Fiction. | Winter—Fiction.
Classification: LCC PZ7.1.S75515 Sil 2020 | DDC [E]—dc23

The text of this book is set in Itsasketch.
The illustrations were rendered in ink, gouache, colored pencils, and love.
Book design by Rachael Cole

MANUFACTURED IN CHINA
2 4 6 8 10 9 7 5 3 1
First Edition